ELEANOR MERRY, CASSANDRA ANGLER, SCOTT DEEGAN, JOSH A. MURPHY, STEPHEN CORDS, DAVID BOWMORE, TINA MERRY, J.B. WOCOSKI, JAMES LIPSON, SHAWN M KLIMEK, MORGAN ADAMS, STEVEN BRUCE, RJ ROLES, BELINDA BRADY, JAMES PYLES, SEA CAUMMISAR, TRISHA MCKEE, NERISHA KEMRAJ, BENJAMIN LANGLEY, MIKE ENNENBACH, DAWN DEBRAAL, AARON BADER, DAVID SIMMS, R.E. SARGENT, ANGELA GLOVER, CHRIS MILLER, DAVID M DONACHIE, KERRI JESMER, WENDY CHEAIRS DAVID M. DONACHIE, TERRY MILLER, JACEK WILKOS, STUART CONOVER, P.J BLAKEY- NOVIS, KEVIN J. KENNEDY, N.M BROWN, SHARON FRAME GAY, GABRIELLA BALCOM, JAY BOWER,

THOMAS STURGEON JR, GABOR EICHAMMER, D.J ELTON, ALANNA WEBB

Dark X-Mas Holiday Drabbles

100 Word Holiday Horror Stories

This novel is entirely a work of fiction. The names, characters and incidents portrayed in it are the work of the author's imagination. Any resemblance to actual persons, living or dead, events or localities is entirely coincidental.

Designations used by companies to distinguish their products are often claimed as trademarks. All brand names and product names used in this book and on its cover are trade names, service marks, trademarks and registered trademarks of their respective owners. The publishers and the book are not associated with any product or vendor mentioned in this book. None of the companies referenced within the book have endorsed the book.

First edition

ISBN: 978- 1- 9992128- 6- 5

Cover art by Brian Scutt

This book was professionally typeset on Reedsy.
Find out more at reedsy.com

Contents

Introduction

Dark X-Mas Holiday Drabbles: 100 Word Horror Stories

From twisted and gory to dark and humorous, these stories have it all. One hundred and twenty three hundred word horror stories, all in the spirit of the season.

With drabbles from: Eleanor Merry, Cassandra Angler, Scott Deegan, Josh A. Murphy, Stephen Cords, David Bowmore, Tina Merry, J.B. Wocoski, James Lipson, Shawn M Klimek, Morgan Adams, Steven Bruce, RJ Roles, Belinda Brady, James Pyles, Sea Caummisar, Trisha McKee, Nerisha Kemraj, Benjamin Langley, Mike Ennenbach, Dawn DeBraal, Aaron Bader, David Simms, R.E. Sargent, Angela Glover, Chris Miller, David M Donachie, Kerri Jesmer, Wendy Cheairs David M. Donachie, Terry Miller, Jacek Wilkos, Stuart Conover, P.J Blakey-Novis, Kevin J. Kennedy, N.M Brown, Sharon Frame Gay, Gabriella Balcom, Jay Bower, Thomas Sturgeon Jr, Gabor Eichammer, D.J Elton, Alanna Robertson-Webb, Drew Starling and more!

I'm Dreaming of a Dark Christmas by Scott Deegan

I'm dreaming of a Dark Christmas
With every little tale that I read
When the knife blades glisten
And scared children listen
To hear slayers in the night
Where sugarplums can be gory
In the frightening elf story
And trees eat favorite household pets
There are gifts on all the pages
Of terror through the ages
Told of gift giving regrets
I'm dreaming of a Dark Christmas
With every little tale I read
While the bright lights shine
And the family dines
In the soft fireplace glow
So hold loved ones tight
It's not Santa visiting tonight
Death lies buried in the snow.

Rudolph's Revenge By Scott Deegan

The barn was eerily quiet when he stepped through the door.

"Hello?" He called. No answer came. He walked farther looking into each stall, finding them empty.

This was wrong.

This was so wrong.

Where was Donner, Blitzen, or Vixen. Vixen wouldn't just leave, not two days before Christmas.

Fear started to creep in, he should go back to his toy shop and find some help. Surely one of his elves knew where the deer were. He turned to see a red glowing nose and blood-soaked antlers.

"Let's play my reindeer games shall we, Santa?" Rudolph lowered his head.

Dyslexia by James Lipson

"…and a Playstation 6, an iPhone 15, a hover board, a new TV…"

"Look kid, I'm not going to tell you again, keep your voice down! And for the last time, I'm not Santa."

"You look like Santa."

"I know, damn it. That's my mistake. I didn't realize the time of year, I thought it might be June or July-ish. No one in their right mind talks to a disheveled, sweaty looking Santa during the summer.

"Your name tag says Santa."

"No, it doesn't. Wait! Billy, is there any chance you have something called Dyslexia?"

"Yes! How did you know?"

Christmas Dinner by Morgan Adams

Hours of combing through Pinterest for the perfect recipe had paid off. Matt leaned over his plate, savoring the exquisite aroma. With near surgical precision, he sliced a razor thin piece of meat then gingerly took a bite. It melted in his mouth in a burst of flavor.

"Mmm, tasty," he murmured.

Smiling in satisfaction, he glanced across the table at his wife. The muscle he'd carved from her chest left a gaping hole of gore. Her dead eyes stared back at him; their superior gleam gone.

"I told you, I'm a better cook than you are. Merry Christmas, darling."

Mother Dear by Cassandra Angler

The wind howled, the cabins windows shaking in their frames. Layers of snow and ice glistening under the pale moonlight. Hands beating against the door, their moans empty and hungry.

They know we're here, the Christmas lights a dead giveaway to the life inside.

Mom just wanted us to be happy, to have one more Christmas like normal. She said the end of the world shouldn't mean the end of Christmas.

She stands now, tied to the stairs railing. Smelling of rotten meat and gnashing her teeth as my sister and I unwrap the gifts that she made for us.

Naughty Dasher by Josh A. Murphy

Jackson spotted them grazing quietly, confused as to why a herd of reindeer were in his local park. *Perhaps they belong to Santa*, he considered, sniggering.

He reached out to pet the smallest of the group.

Without warning, the reindeer clumsily swiped its head in the boy's direction, sharp antlers impaling his throat.

He let out a gargled scream before collapsing into the cold, wet snow.

Zipping up his fly, Santa emerged from behind the tree and watched the boy bleed out.

'Not again, Dasher!' he cursed, jumping back into his sleigh and hastily fleeing the scene of the crime.

Christmas Morning By Kerri Jesmer

Christmas morning and the children hadn't awakened her. The sun was well up in the sky and a blanket of snow, untouched, covered the ground outside her window. As she lay there listening, she noticed the odd sounds coming from downstairs.

Something was wrong.

She threw on her robe and slippers and headed down the stairs. She passed her children's room and saw they were not there. As the living room began to be visible, she saw three small bodies run away from the tree. They were not her children.

"Kids?" she called. Little demons, bloodied teeth gnashing, answered her.

Santa's Workshop by Trisha McKee

It was a rare treat. To be given a tour of what had once been Santa's workshop. Everyone missed Christmas, and they especially missed Santa.

The parents were ordered to wait outside, as this was for the children after all. But as the children walked through the empty workshops and saw the shattered model cars, the screaming doll babies, and the rotten gumdrops dripping from the walls, their excitement turned to disappointment. And as they were led to the naughty or nice conference room where the corpse of Santa waited with a chilling, toothless smile, their disappointment turned to terror.

It's A Bad Thing by Aaron Bader

"I can't believe I'm saying this Martha, but... this fruitcake is absolutely phenomenal! What's your secret?".

Martha smiled from ear to ear over Jane's gleeful reaction. She spent the last ten years dedicated to defeat the festive holiday stereotype of fruitcake.

"Please Martha I beg you, how did you make it!?".

Martha performed an innocent smile.

"I'm sorry Jane, keeping that hidden will win me this year's fall fair".

Jane pouted, "Well, it's absolutely to die for Martha".

"It certainly is Jane."

Nobody saw the trail of blood, or heard the screaming coming from her basement.

Christmas Vacation by Shawn Klimek

The first human step on Venus's blistering surface by Major Carlisle had required many inventions, including a spacesuit able to withstand caustic smog, forge-like temperatures, and pulverizing atmospheric pressure and a timely accident sidelining the astronaut originally slated for the historic honor.

Fortunately, Colonel Bristol had shown no resentment. Carlisle chuckled to recall his witty farewell from the orbiting command module, "See you after Christmas." Bristol's joke was that the 224-day, Venusian, calendar ends August 13th.

Aiming his face towards the hellish skies, Carlisle presented an appreciative salute.

Slowly, it dawned on him that Bristol was no longer in orbit.

A Partridge in a Pear Tree by J. B. Wocoski

Peter Partridge climbed a pear tree to end it all quick and clean. However, his rope was way too long, landing him safely on the ground over and over again.

He got it right one last time, but his toe tips barely touching the ground. He died slowly gasping and choking to late to regret it all. The note in his pocket blew away before Christmas Day.

As he hung around, the hungry ravens fed on his remains. Crows stripped his flesh clean away as his white ash bones hung there chiming in the wind tolling this morbid Christmas Carol.

Among Elves and Other Nasty Deeds by RJ Roles

Jecko's official title was 'Chief Maintenance Elf,' meaning that he was a glorified janitor. Jecko didn't mind the work, but he only wanted to be one of the toy makers. Hanso never let Jecko forget what a pitiful elf he was, especially in front of others.

Fed up beyond the breaking point, Jecko plotted his revenge. One of his tasks was to feed the reindeer everyday. Purposely neglecting them for a week, they were ravenous.

"Santa? Jecko said you wanted to see me."

The reindeer fell upon the unsuspecting elf as Jecko watched from above, his eyes alight with glee.

Carniverous Coniferous by Aaron Bader

The perfect tree fell after Templeton's final swing made its claim. The promise he made to his family had to be kept. Night had fallen quickly.

Trudging through the dark, his worst fear was realized as his flashlight flickered into failure.

"Damnit!", he cursed.

A creepy green light he hadn't noticed, shone from the woods to his left.

A short walk to the source revealed a magnificent tree covered in decorations. Templeton stood there hypnotized by its beauty. His arms felt heavy. His legs wouldn't budge, as he stood there smiling. The tree's roots pulled his enveloped body forward.

Icy- Cold Karma by Gabriella Balcom

Ray gestured at the creek and thin rivulets of water rose from the surface, streaming toward him.

They froze in his hand, forming spears. He called more liquid to him, transformed it into an ice bat and bullets and hid behind some bushes.

Caden swaggered along. Although Christmas was only days away, he'd fired Ray yesterday, taking credit for his work. Caden hadn't cared that his employee had a family to support.

Ray batted ice bullets toward his former boss, who gasped as they struck.

Making the spears zoom toward the other man, Ray then spat on Caden's motionless body.

The Christmas Ad by Trisha McKee

Little Susie showed her mother the ad in the paper. "I can send Santa my Christmas list!" This ad even promised a letter from Santa in return. So Susie got to work on writing out her list. She included a picture of herself, her age, her name, and her address, just as the ad requested. Her mother even helped her address the letter and put a stamp on it.

And when they received the letter, Diane and Frank looked over the picture. "Oh, this girl would be a great addition to our family. I'd like to have her before Christmas."

Christmas Tree by Jacek Wilkos

I stood in the middle of the room, watching my work with pride. I made a Christmas tree from angels. Wings imitating branches grew from the trunk made from bones. I decorated the tree with Christmas balls made from skulls and a chain of intestines. Blond hair of Cherubs twisted together in threads sparkled in the warm light of candles. I even made small finger-bones pentagrams.

The desecration of Christmas is a tradition in our home. This year it was my turn to decorate the Christmas tree.

I hope father Azazel and mother Naamah will be proud of me.

One Surprise That Christmas Eve by Terry Miller

The fire roared in the fireplace, the chimney expelling the grey smoke into the crisp, wintry air. Kelly Holdren slept on a warm, bearskin rug, her best friend Roxy made a cozy, furry pillow.

Kelly jolted awake at the sound of a slamming door.

"Mom? Dad?" She inquired to no answer.

Her parents' bedroom door was shut, all was quiet. She opened the door and peered inside.

The window stood wide open, snow blowing furiously inside. On the white yard below, her parents stood; each with a corncob pipe, eyes black as coal, and the snow sticking head to toe.

The Stockings Were Hung by Morgan Adams

Christmas was supposed to be the most magical morning of the year. Billy wanted everything to be perfect, but his parents had forgotten the stockings. He'd warned them, if things weren't perfect, there'd be hell to pay.

A fire crackled in the hearth. The presents were wrapped in shiny foil and placed under the tree. Lights flickered, ornaments sparkled, and fresh cocoa had been made. Billy hung his mother's head on the mantle using the green garland. His father's head dangled next to hers.

They were hung by the chimney with care.

Sometimes you had to make sacrifices for perfection.

The Giving Season (Part 1) By Stephen Cords

The smiling man made his way past the bell ringing Santa and slid a small wrapped gift into the man's pot.

"Hope this helps."

"Ho-Ho-Ho! Bless you, sir."

The man didn't acknowledge the thanks or break his stride. He continued down the street, smiling.

Last year he had anonymously made the news by dropping his victim's jewelry into kettles around the city. Everyone had been so happy. He couldn't wait to see what the reporters would have to say about this year's donations.

"One down, nine to go."

He sang 'Here Comes Santa Claus' quietly to himself and walked on.

The Biggest Package by Kerri Jesmer

The box arrived Christmas Eve. Boone could hardly lift it to place beside the tree as something inside shifted. He returned to his drink and downed another.

Christmas morning, he heard the screams in his stupor of sleep and alcohol but could not rouse himself. Hours later, when he finally made his way downstairs, he saw a bloodied family room.

He ran through the house, calling their names, finding pieces of their bodies here and there. Then he saw the dark figure crouched in the corner and heard a low growl. The last sound he heard was his own screams.

I Hope It Hurt by Cassandra Angler

I hope it hurt.

The way I hung you from the chimney.

I hope it hurt.

My arm reaching down your throat, pulling out your organs one by one. I hope the darkness came slowly, the Christmas carols that played forever tainted with your suffering. You look quite refined against the blinking tree lights. A unique addition to my stocking collection.

I hope it hurt.

Knowing that you meant nothing to me. That your life faded without meaning. Santa says he's proud as he marvels my work. Your hollow corpse will hold so many goodies and treats.

I hope it hurt.

Hooves by Chris Miller

"You hear it, daddy?" I asked, breathless.

He said nothing, looking at the ceiling.

"What—"

"It's Santa and his reindeer!"

But he wasn't smiling. His face was white.

"Kara!" he shouted as he fetched the shotgun by the door.

"Get Ronnie and hide!"

I was confused. Why was daddy upset about Santa coming? He's the one who'd told me about him.

My mother grabbed me, pulling towards the closet. The crack of the shotgun and my daddy's scream stopped us.

We froze, seeing the spattered spot by the door and the furry leg with its hoof in the blood.

The Family Cabin by Angela Glover

As they licked their fingers clean, Abby smiled knowing Christmas dinner was successful. Luke was startled when I came out of the snowy woods barefoot with a bloody nightgown. As he ushered me into the cabin, another young girl appeared, and he told her to find a blanket.

Looking for injuries, he realized I was neither hurt nor cold.

Looking into his eyes, I smiled as she pushed the fire iron through his skull.

See, I wasn't lost in the woods and she is my sister. Luke rented our family cabin for some fun and we're always hungry for predators.

Guide by Sleigh Tonight by James Lipson

"I'm not sure he can do it again."

"You said that last year and the year before that. Let's do our job, reprehensible as it may be, and go home."

"Come on Herbie, look at him. He can't stand, he has emphysema and is virtually blind in both eyes. Every year we have to do this. Why? Someone has to put a stop to this, it's inhumane."

"I agree, they should have let him retire years ago, but they didn't. It's what Santa wants, it's Christmas and there's a blizzard, so give me the bourbon and funnel. Now where's Rudolph?"

In the Woods by Gabriella Balcom

"You're lying," Lindsey accused. "They aren't in the woods."

"Yes, they are," her sister Ann insisted. "I bet they came because it's Christmas eve."

The girls crept into the forest, hiding behind some trees.

Hoofbeats soon rang out. Dozens of reindeer dashed into the nearby clearing, prancing around and kicking up their heels.

"Wow," Lindsey whispered wide-eyed.

"Told you," Ann replied.

But the animals' flesh began melting from their bodies. Loping toward the horrified girls, their eyes glowed red.

Lindsey and Ann panicked and fled, screaming as loudly as they could.

Their cries stopped after the skeletal reindeer caught them.

The Giving Season (Part 2) by Stephen Cords

The beast skulked around the corner of the house. "Too early", it thought. "Not safe here for days yet."

It smelled smoke from the fireplace and pine. Shadows danced on the drifts in front of the windows, inviting him inside where he knew he would find... A long, low growl escaped his throat. "No. Not here."

It smelled the children, freshly washed and bedded down. Innocent. Vulnerable.

It left the offering on the mat, scratched the door and bolted for the trees.

Carolyn opened the door and saw the bloody deer's leg. "Merry Christmas, David. Come back to us soon."

Tinsel Tannenbaum by Dawn DeBraal

The tree was trimmed with tinsel.
　Oh, so shining bright.
　Then my doggy Skippy,
　ate it in the night.

Waking the next morning.
　I had a sense of dread.
　Skippy didn't bark no more,
　Skippy now was dead.

The tree went out the door
　My father had some words,
　But now the tinsel was a threat
　To all the little birds.

They liked the shining glory
　They choked, and they stopped
　flying
　It truly was so gory
　To see the birds all dying.

The tree then toppled over
　Rolling to its side.
　Electrical conduit

The tree blew up and fried.

Death of the Fat Man by M Ennenbach

The fire roars, flames licking the blackened hearth. Sparks travel up the chimney to dance momentarily in the frozen air like fireflies. Red and blue lights flash against the virgin snowfall, a myriad cast in crystalline reflection. A trail of red, black in the night, steaming into the woods.

In the house the responding officer vomits into a festive tin of popcorn decorated with stockings and a spray of blood. In the fireplace, the sizzle of flesh and charred bone fills the room with the stench of cooking meat and burnt hair. Wisps of red velvet and leather boots smoldering.

The Present Still Wrapp'd by Benjamin Langley

On the twelfth day of Christmas, when removing decorations from the tree, Herbert discovered it: an unopened present hidden among the lower branches. Alas, the tag was missing, so Herbert knew not for whom it was intended.

The children were out, so he made the eternally regrettable decision to open the gift. The delicate paper fell open as he pulled open the bow.

What he saw sent him into a pit of despair from which he may never escape and had surely been sent by the devil himself – who else was capable of such evil? Socks, odd to begin with.

Wassel by Chris Miller

"Delicious, baby," he said and sipped, wincing at the heat.

"No one makes Wassel like you."

She smiled, winked.

"Not like me," she said, chuckling. "I experimented with the recipe."

His eyes rose.

"Is that right? I thought there was something different."

"Like it?"

"Mmm," he hummed, taking another sip. "I do. Is that almonds? Wonderful addition, honey."

"Thought you'd like it," she said, her smile fading.

His eyes narrowed at her. Then his throat began to narrow.

He choked.

"Honey?"

She crossed her arms, smiling.

"Not honey," she said. "And not almonds, though I hear it tastes like them."

Hells Bells by David Bowmore

The bell ringers played the town centre every Christmas. The handheld brass bells played an infernal, high-pitched racket that drove deep into one's brain. It was maddening.

People dropped coins in the bucket so they wouldn't play. And it wasn't enough that they assaulted passers by; they also went house to house.

Every year, they made the long trek up to the secluded farmhouse. And every year the farmer sent them away again with harsh un-Christian words.

This year, they refused to listen. Instead, they surrounded him with noise until his ears bled.

He would never hear anything else again.

The Slasher by Gabriella Balcom

The woman lay on the ground face-up, her throat slashed. Underneath her closed eyelids, police found carved X's in her eyes. Deep stab wounds covered her torso, her stomach gaping open. Her intestines and esophagus had been positioned around her body in the shape of a Christmas tree.

After Detectives Bunton and Twayer arrived, Bunton plodded around, studying everything while Twayer made a sketch.

"No evidence anywhere," Bunton announced. "Not a drop of blood either."

Twayer nodded. "She was killed elsewhere and positioned here."

"Just like the others. Every Christmas, the Slasher does the same thing with a new victim."

The Twelfth Day by Tina Merry

On the 1st day of Christmas, my true love left me, and the world went dark.

On the second day of Christmas, *they* came.

On the third day of Christmas, I knew fear.

On the 4th day of Christmas, I ran.

On the 5th day, I hid.

On the 6th day, I knew hunger.

On the 7th day, I wept.

On the 8th day, I accepted.

On the 9th day, I fought.

On the 10th day, I despaired.

On the 11th day, I died.

On the 12th day of Christmas, I was reborn, and my true love came to me.

Blood Drunk by Terry Miller

There's blood on the snow, resembling a delicious snocone. It looked delicious. Derrick grabbed a handful, lapping up the metallic flavor. Upstairs, in the house, he heard screams harmonize like a sweet carol sung in the spirit of the season. His smile gleamed in the streetlight, his tongue moving hungrily over lusting fangs.

Derrick's comrades exited the house, swaying in drunken swagger. He nodded as they met in the street. Arm in arm, they gleefully turned the corner; their sights focused upon a new row of houses. The night was still young and there was more to drink.

Much more.

Watching by Drew Starling

Chloe rubbed her little eyes at the breakfast table. Another sleepless December night. "The black eyes," again, "watching me sleep".

Julie didn't know how to respond. Chloe had the same nightmare last year – every night for three weeks last December. Here it was again.

So that night, Julie went to Chloe's room. She wanted to see for herself –and –she saw –

The family's Christmas nutcrackers, usually decorated throughout the house, were all circled around Chloe's bed. Their eyes glowing, black, watching the child. And there was Chloe, sitting up, waiting, her eyes also glowing black.

"Hi mommy. We're watching you."

Christmas Came Too Early by Stuart Conover

No one knew what happened to Randolph.
It had been a snowy Halloween.
He was last seen setting up Christmas decorations.
Long into the night he toiled away.
Yet in the morning he was gone.
Sparkling lights covered the lawn in an elaborate pattern.
Snowmen stood at each point.
At the center, a giant present had appeared.
It really was an elaborate piece.
Yet the creator was missing.
Most suspected an unannounced vacation.
Months passed.
After Christmas an investigation began.
The police finally unwrapped the present.
Within, the body of Randolph.
Only his head was missing.
Replaced with a jack-o-lantern.

The Naughty List by RJ Roles

Jingle bells ringing drew Danny out of his slumber. He rose out of bed, creeping down the hallway toward the cheery bell sounds. Danny giggled into his hands, suspecting he was about to reveal his parents stuffing the space beneath the tree full of presents.

Shocked horror ran through his mind when he saw the source of the jingles.

"Hello, Danny."

Santa took a bite of cookie, following Danny's gaze to his parents, who were hanging from the hearth.

"They were on my naughty list." He rose to his feet. "Oh my, Danny."

*Tsk*Tsk*Tsk*

Danny ran in terror.

The Cruel Snowman by Thomas Sturgeon Jr

His vengeance is as cold as ice and yet here he kills again. Sending shard's of ice into the

Heart of the helpless victim not realizing the hazard at hand. Jealous of the humans blood. The Snowman seizes it. Draining it into himself.

Knowing that he can't be like the human race with the warmth of life. That it makes him envy every human on the planet. His next victim to attack is on Christmas day, eyeing his target,

Following her home. Hoping to make her blood a lot less warmer. He was cruel at heart, his days were numbered.

The White Hunt by Gábor Eichammer

When he was eight, Ove wanted one thing for Christmas - a rifle. He got a bicycle instead.

Bitterly disappointed in Santa, he swore vengeance. By thirty, Ove had bought his own rifle. A skilled tracker, he hunted and stalked the cold north.

One Christmas Eve, he saw strange lights fill the sky. He found wide boot tracks, heard the hearty belly laugh: Ho-ho-ho!

Hands shaking, Ove aimed his rifle at something red glowing between the pines. A great reindeer grunted and charged. Ove's weapon misfired, the barrel frozen with fear. Rudolph protected his master and Ove's last present was death.

Soot by Chris Miller

She blinked, not believing. It was too soon. She hadn't meant it, her letter. She'd just wanted the doll. But they'd said no, and she was mad.

But the sooty footprints were unmistakable.

She followed the footprints, knowing where they would lead, praying she was wrong.

"Mom?" she called tremulously.

Nothing.

The footprints ended at her parents room and she pushed open the door.

His suit was black, not red. But as she began to scream, she noticed that his beard was red.

Just like her parents's opened throats.

"Joy to the world!" he howled cheerily. "The deed is done!"

First Signs of a Serial Killer by Sea Caummisar

The five year old boy worked hard on the candy cane, all day.

Each lick and suck of the candy served its purpose. Even though he didn't care for peppermint, he knew it had to be done.

His mother sat him on Santa's lap, so he could tell him his wish list.

He had no list. Instead, the young boy stabbed Santa with the sharp shaped point he chiseled on the candy stick.

All he wanted was to see Santa bleed.

He was sad when the candy broke and barely punctured Santa's skin.

Abduction by David M. Donachie

Little Timmy's fear of aliens extended to Father Christmas. This year he was determined to avoid abduction at any costs, which he reckoned might involve being dragged up the chimney by extraterrestrial elves. The house's one remaining fireplace had a gas fire which no longer worked, so he blocked it up with paper to keep out any jolly descending reptoids. Sadly, Brian didn't know about Timmy's fear when he decided to fix the fire and put it on to impress the family on Christmas Eve.

The police said that they had been 'stolen away in the night' by carbon monoxide.

Best Present Ever by P.J. Blakey-Novis

On Christmas morning I ran to the living room. The tree stood unlit, surrounded by gifts. Desperate to open them, I ran to my parents' room. Even in the darkness I could tell Dad wasn't there. I shook Mum awake and she smiled. "Where's Dad?" I asked, indifferent to his absence. Mum looked confused. "I'm not sure, he was out last night. Again."

It would be another week before his bloated corpse would be found in the chimney, a soot-covered Santa hat on his head. Had he tried being festive, or was he simply a drunken fool?

Probably the latter.

Under the Mantel, With Care by David Simms

Breath scrambles from lung, to lips, back to lung
  The bodies slide down the walls to press against me
  Burning away my hope of scampering up the sides
  My fingers falter along the smooth surface
  The killer tossed me away after choosing my fate
  The light fading, with all hope blackened
  I prayed for hours for a helping hand, a cry for help unanswered
  With each scream, others pile upon, the dread of the coming morn
  Awaiting the tear from the crypt pressed upon us like rocks dropping deep
  Into the stocking of the child come sunrise, steals another life.

The Giving Season (Part 3) by Stephen Cords

She kissed her lover deeply. "If that's what I get coming through the door, I can't wait to unwrap my present."

She smiled at him. "I have a surprise. Everything is set up and waiting."

The woman took his hand and led him to a door. "Merry Christmas, Vincent," she said.

He turned and looked at her questioningly. "I'm Mark."

The woman kicked his right knee and shoved him down the stairs to the basement.

A hulking form separated itself from the shadows and stepped into the light.

"Thank you, mother. This is much better than the puppy last year."

Ice Queen by Sharon Fame Gay

In my yard is a snowman. It was late last night when I built it. In a moment of artistic clarity, I added a scarf and hat, something to ward off the bitter freeze. I tied the scarf gently, wiped away the ice from sightless eyes peering out from the frosty head.

The scarf was a vivid blue, one I'd found in the dresser drawer, a silken thing I gave as a gift last year. She should have returned it to the store. Red is more her color.

It will be a long winter. They won't find her until spring.

Spoilt Brat by David Bowmore

All I wanted for Christmas was a new bike.

The bike I use now is old, too small to ride properly, and knackered.

But, did I get a what I wanted? No, they got me a puppy. I'm thirteen, not five.

The sort of puppy that girls get given. It had a ribbon tied up in a bow on top of her

head. They called her Poppy.

Poppy!

And they expect me to pick up her poop – FFS.

This is the worst Christmas ever.

I'll get them for this. I know, I'll bake them a cake. A dog poop cake.

Hark! Nate Carols And Jessica Screams
by Terry Miller

Beneath the tree, Jessica shivered. Stark naked, the fireplace did little to warm her pale skin. Nate descended the stairs, his eyes on his present all the way down. Her young, twenty-year-old flesh was even more appealing beneath the lights and garland.

Nate brought a knife from the kitchen, a little help opening up a package never hurt. He knelt, tracing her thigh with the blade as he admired her; then he opened his gift. The crimson streams flowed from Jessica's gushing wounds, Nate finger-painted lyrics of carols upon the walls.

Hark the herald angels sing, he wrote with glee.

Taking What I Want by Gabriella Balcom

"All I wanted for Christmas was blood," Tyanne told the man. "Santa didn't bring me any, but yours will do."

"What is this?" he demanded. "A stupid Christmas prank?"

Tyanne chuckled and licked her lips.

"Get lost, wacko." He snorted when she grinned, revealing her fangs. But his eyes widened when she moved toward him so fast that her body blurred.

"Run for me, will you? I love that." She reveled in his fear.

He backed away, then ran.

Quickly catching up, Tyanne pinned him to a tree with one hand around his throat, and laughed.

A Ring for Christmas by Dawn DeBraal

It was supposed to be the gift of all gifts. Robert hinted she was getting a "ring" for Christmas. Bernita tried not to go through the closets. She turned her eyes away if she spotted anything wrapped in holiday paper. On Christmas morning she waited under the tree. It was strange that Robert wasn't there. Bernita wondered where Robert could, be? Did the store make her gift the wrong size? She answered her cell phone.

"Hello?"

"It's me, Robert."

"Robert, where are you?"

"It doesn't matter, I've left you. This is the only "ring" you'll get from me for Christmas."

The Perfect Snowman by Sea Caummisar

All she needed was a Santa hat to top her perfect snowman.

She glanced at the blue eyes, which she plucked from her husband's head.

The nose looked like it was running, but instead of snot it was blood.

From where she cut it from her husband's face.

The smile didn't look very friendly since the severed lips turned pale and frozen.

Her husband had been moving when she sliced the meat from around his mouth.

So the cuts were jagged.

After adding the Santa hat, it was perfect.

Her husband would never cheat on her again.

Peace Comes From Blood by Jay Bower

When I was eight, my mom gave me what she thought was the greatest Christmas present: a brown teddy bear. Don't get me wrong, bears are cool and all, but the best gift? I didn't even think so when I was a kid! What she gave me instead was a curse.

To this day Mr. Giggles lives with me.

He needs blood. Always more blood. If I refuse? He takes mine, but I have no more to give.

So I kill for him. I kill for me. Mr. Giggles needs his food and I need peace. Peace comes from blood.

An Oral History Of Santa by Stuart Conover

Everyone wants to talk about Rudolph. The truth of the matter is that red nosed bastard didn't last a year.

A hunter saw his glow and took a shot that put out his light for good. The only two reindeer who have lasted are Donner and Blitzen.

Good old Lightning and Thunder have been Santa's true enforcers for decades. You think the Donner Party was about cannibalism? Humans didn't eat each other in Nevada that year.

It wasn't their first taste of man meat, nor their last.

If you mess with Claus, those are the two he sends after you.

Fruitcake Exchange by Sharon Fame Gay

The whole neighborhood would remember Edith this year, she thought. She slaved away in the kitchen, aromas wafting out into the street, a combination of fruit and nut in a glorious batter that look like tiny jewels. She removed each cake from the pan and wrapped them in cellophane.

Then she toted each one through the snow and left them on doorsteps or placed in mail boxes along with a cheerful note. How was Edith to know her neighbors hated fruitcake? All that rat poison, gone to waste.

But, down at the mission, at least half a dozen people died.

One Shift Too Many by Kevin J. Kennedy

One Thousand, seven hundred and forty years Santa had been doing his job.
In the beginning he loved that he brought joy to children.

After a thousand years he liked the fact that he only worked once a year. After
fifteen hundred years he only liked that Mrs Clause didn't age.

After seventeen hundred years, he hated the job completely.

Forty years after that, he liked the way the blood splattered on the walls of
the toy factory as he slaughtered the elves mercilessly.

"Ho fucking ho," he screamed as he danced between them, swinging a candy
cane like scythe.

The Keepsake by Shawn Klimek

Dad reached under the Christmas to retrieve the first gift.

"This one is for Eric," he said, "...from Mom."

Eric sobbed. "I miss her!"

"And one for you, Elmo," he continued, "...also from Mom."

Elmo bawled. "I wish she were here!"

"We all do!" Dad soothed, giving Edna a sharp look, "That's why we never play with matches."

Finally, he turned to his daughter. "I'm sorry, Edna," he said. "Your gift burned up with Mom in the fire. Never mind. She would have wanted you to have this keepsake."

Without even looking, Edna knew it was a lump of coal.

Xander's First Christmas by Angela Glover

Adrienne's eyes shot open to the sound of muffled crying. Glancing at the clock on her nightstand, it was just past midnight, but she padded her way in the dark. Xander needed to be held and he loves to watch the twinkling lights on the Christmas tree.

She hummed "Silent Night" as they sat in the rocker, but John woke Xander by yanking him from her arms. Adrienne shrieked, "he'll miss his first Christmas again!"

John sadly shook his head as he called Dr. Bronson.

Mother of Invention by James Lipson

"Are you suggesting we actually stop him?"

"I am. I'm tired of him making us look bad in front of our kids. I can't keep up with HIM, none of us can."

"Are you telling us something we don't know, Jedidiah?"

"I am not. What I am telling you is we need to stop competing with him, it's a never-ending battle we can't win. But, if we eliminate his access, we eliminate the problem, don't we?"

"Yes. But that means we would have to seal our fireplaces shut in the winter."

"No. It doesn't. May I present the Amish Fireplace."

Fairy Lights by David M. Donachie

"It'll be a nice surprise when he gets home from work," Julie thought.

She dragged a chair over to the windows, then drew the curtains. She'd got a string of fairy lights from the charity shop and planned to hang them along the curtain rail. The first half was easy, but she couldn't make the last bit stay up. She stretched, stood on tip-toe, reached with her fingers. The chair wobbled; slipped; shot out from under her! She snatched at the curtain rail, but it wasn't the curtain that stopped her fall.

When Martin got home, the surprise wasn't nice.

You Did What? by James Lipson

"Please tell me you're joking?"

"I'm not. Like I told you, I had my stomach stapled over the summer. What do you think?"

"What do I think? What do I think! I think I'm looking at a silly old man desperately clinging to a past that has long since abandoned him. I think I'm looking at someone who is making his wife miserable. And I'm 100% positive I'm looking at someone who is, selfishly, going to disappoint billions of children come Christmas time. That's what I think."

"Brenda in accounting said I look good."

"Kris, Brenda says everyone looks good."

The Belnicklers by David Simms

They burst through the door without song, only the masks, the sacks, and what they held in their hands. Our heritage pursued us into the new world, into the mountains of the land across the ocean. Krampus lay forgotten, his nightmares tucked back in the snows of the Alps. My family survived, escaped and reborn. Unscathed.

Yet he sent his minions, costumed to disguise. Sent for me. The sinner. You can't outrun sins, one said through the grotesque hood, unsheathing his switch snapping it against the floor.

Welcome home, it said.

When he opened the sack, my screams drowned out the night.

The Santa Trap by Benjamin Langley

All Alfie wanted was proof that Santa existed.

    The plan was simple: a tripwire attached to a bell would alert him, and he'd run in with his phone and take a picture.

    But sometimes, even at Christmas, you don't get what you want.

    He heard the bell and raced into the living room. That's when he saw how tragically wrong it had all gone.

    Santa wasn't supposed to really trip on the wire.

    Santa wasn't supposed to hit his head. He'd taken the picture before he realised what had happened.

    Now he had proof alright – proof that Santa had existed.

The Nutcracker by R.E. Sargent

Christmas always confused me. I never understood how a fat man could fit down our chimney.

When I was seven, I decided I needed to know the truth. I snuck out of bed while my parents were in the other room and hid behind the couch. It wasn't long before I saw Mommy and Santa come into the living room together and sit on the couch. They started kissing and Santa grabbed Mom's boob. I jumped from my hiding spot and smashed Santa in the nuts.

Mom says I'm the reason I can't have a brother or sister for Christmas.

A Bad Child by Sea Caummisar

A trail of bloody gingerbread cookies led the young girl to her prizes.

Waking up Christmas Day was always so exciting.

Every year, Santa left behind the best presents.

The green Christmas tree was now red, covered with a sticky liquid.

Full of vigor, the girl didn't want to wait for her parents to wake up.

She opened the first box and her Mother's head was inside, scary blank eyes staring back into her own. Krampus appeared behind her, holding up his bloody claws, grinning wide and showing his pointed red teeth.

"Were you naughty this year?"

Shaggy Killed Christmas by Nerisha Kemraj

Gladys smiled as her next-door-neighbors entered for Christmas Dinner.

"Thanks for the invite, Gladys. We were surprised, considering what happened last week."

"It's ok, Jill. Accidents happen." Gladys took their coats.

"Yeah, these cats are another story. He shouldn't have ran in front of my car. Stupid animal," Roger retorted.

Anger flashed in her eyes, as Gladys gave them their drinks.

After dinner, the Smiths bade goodbye, renewed friendship in their hearts.

"Merry Christmas, and thank you for coming."

She closed the door, smirking. Soon, the untraceable poison would take effect. She hugged the picture of her beloved cat, Shaggy.

Twas The Night by Alanna Robertson-Webb

I left my siblings on the roof last night, and when our mother found them this morning she wouldn't stop wailing. Getting them up there was easy, and kicking the ladder away was fun.

Mom was too drunk to notice what I had done last night, and even when they screamed for me to let them down I refused.

Now their pajama-clad, frozen corpses look like storybook snowmen, and maybe this will make Mom think twice before she asks me to read those brats Twas the Night Before Christmas while they throw beer bottles at my head.

Merry Christmas everyone!

Class Christmas List by N.M. Brown

The students passed their papers in towards the front of the class to be collected. There were so many adorable Christmas lists; almost every student illustrated theirs.

One list was smeared in black crayon. There were no words; only a drawing of a broken baby-doll at the bottom of her paper. Its eyes were marked with X's. It laid in a red crayon pool of blood.

She never returned from Christmas break. After making an inquiry, I was told the family moved due to a tragedy. They'd lost their two-month-old son; death ruled accidental.

Quiet by Cassandra Angler

Sally ran down the stairs, excited, giddy. The house still quiet. Everyone else must still be sleeping, she thought as she tip toed into the living room. The tree was lit, the underneath stuffed with presents. She gasped, and clapped her hands. As she watched the blinking lights, a steady thumping came from one of the wrapped gifts. "A puppy," she said into the emptiness, "Must be wagging his tail". She picked it up, the bottom wet and sticky.

Eagerly she ripped the paper away, and lifted the lid. She screamed, backing away. Laying in tissue paper, a beating heart.

The Red Drip by by Gábor Eichammer

Chimneys are a thing of the past - it's all central heating and brass pipes now. Yet the children must still be served.

My goal is clear - there's no time to disrobe. I can't even remove my boots. I start to dissolve, my belly melting and my eyes liquefying. I slip into the small hole on the roof. For a brief moment my glove is the same thing as my ear. I drip out from the warm radiator like an IV into a dying man's arm. I am a red pool of joy on the floor. The children must be served.

O, Angelic Messenger by Terry Miller

The angel sat atop the tree, impaled with bleeding slowed to but a trickle. How she got to the top was a feat of strength surely not her own, the pine must've stood twenty feet high.

An old Halloween costume, a hand-me-down from her cousins, she'd decided to wear it for the church's Christmas play. A lover of children, she was always eager to help out. This time, though, they weren't children at all but rebellious elves. Agreeing to send a message to ol' Mr.Kringle, they chose her as their messenger. It was a message delivered loud and clear.

Holiday Memories by Shawn Klimek

Richard reached across the passenger seat and unlocked the door. "Get in," he told the hag.

She hesitated, licking her gums.

"Let me see it, first."

From a pocket, Richard withdrew the baggy containing a white crystal and shook it in front of her sunken eyes. They flared greedily. She got in and pulled the door shut.

"What do you want for it?" she asked.

He put the meth back into his pocket. "You'll see."

They drove across town before parking outside a large mansion. Just within, four children were waiting.

"Merry Christmas kids," he said, "Your mother is home."

Panto by David Bowmore

During the festive season, theatres up and down the land stage pantomimes; the origins of which date back many hundreds of years.

Essentially, men dress as ugly sisters and women play handsome princes, while recounting fairy-tales tinged with innuendo for the adults and slapstick for the kiddies.

Audience participation is essential.

"Oh no it isn't!"

Last year's show will live long in the memory.

You see, Buttons and Cinders had once been intimate – off stage, naturally.

She shouldn't have taunted him publicly.

He shouldn't have slashed her face with the glass slipper, while chanting the line,

"Let's do it again!"

I Know by Marie Chambers and Drew Starling

Closing the door, tipsy, she says, "It was a good party, as holiday parties go."

She's more distant than usual tonight. I know why, and it's about to come out.

She's jittery. "There's eggnog left. Have a glass?"

She pours. Generously. Two glasses. "Cinnamon?"

"Yes, darling." I sprinkle it in both.

She sips. And speaks. "I— cheated. I mean— I am. Now. Cheating."

I smile. Sad, but compliant.

She pleads. "I'm so— I'm sor—"

"—sshhhhh." I stop her. "I know."

She's crying, confused, eggnog and cinnamon on her lip.

Then – she coughs. She lurches. She falls.

She's dead.

To Grandmothers House We Go by R.E. Sargent

My parents packed the station wagon with the things we would need to spend the night at our Grandparent's house. It had snowed all day and being Christmas eve, we wanted to make sure we didn't get stranded at home.

We all jumped into the car and headed out of town, taking the bridge over the vast river before turning onto a road that would take us through the mysterious woods. We drove up as Grandmother was tucking something under the porch. I peeked later.

An axe?

Grandfather never joined us for dinner. In fact, we never saw him again.

Was I Bad? by Wendy Cheairs

I did terrible things, stole, lies, and cheated.

I won when I should have lost, I took what was not mine, and never was caught.

Does that make me wrong?

I think not.

Holidays came and out shopping with money, not mine one of the small dirty children asking for money told me I was doomed. I laughed, drove away and kicking up muck. I woke on Christmas morning to get everything I wanted, except there were no gifts this year. Only a goat demon in my living room eating through my guest laughing at my plight.

Krampus is real?

You're Not Santa! by P.J. Blakey-Novis

At fourteen I was beyond believing in Santa and could no longer be bribed into behaving. I was a terror and didn't care. I'd been especially horrible Christmas Eve; teasing my siblings, ignoring Mum, yet still expecting gifts to be waiting in the morning. At 3am I was awoken by a sound; footsteps perhaps, but more…animalistic. Through my bedroom door came a snort, followed by the door swinging open. With hooves instead of hands and feet, and vicious horns upon its head, the creature growled.

"You're not Santa!" I whimpered.

"Santa's for the good children," Krampus replied, before he attacked.

Day Of Reckoning by Eleanor Merry

Pushing through the chaos I take a deep breath, steeling myself in preparation for what's to come. I'm armed, and ready as I'll ever be to take on this madness. Why I didn't do this sooner, before the level of destruction and greed was at its highest, I don't know. Perhaps fear held me back, perhaps something else.

I squeeze my eyes shut and whisper one final prayer, hoping someone up there likes me enough to see me through today.

Opening my eyes, I swallow hard and push through the doors and into the abyss.

I fucking hate Christmas shopping.

Sweet Tooth Saint Lussi by David Bowmore

Lussi smelled sweet like sugar coated fruit, had the brightest eyes, the sweetest smile and wore spectacles that hung around her neck on a fine chain.

After school, children would barge through the door of her sweet shop - eager for their hit. Kind, polite, rude and naughty, even the ones who tried to swipe an extra bar - she welcomed them all.

But at Christmas, she would begin her true work.

Saint Lussi would bundle special children into a sack, dragging them home to work her magic – the rendering of fat and bone.

Naughty children had the sweetest taste.

Rudolph the Bloody Nosed Reindeer by Sea Caummisar

Rudolph the bloody nosed reindeer.

Had such a bloody nose.

And if you ever saw it, you would even say it shows.

All of the other reindeer used to hit him and call him names.

That's why poor bloody Rudolph made up his own reindeer games.

Then one foggy Christmas Eve, Santa came to say

"Rudolph with your broken nose so bloody, do you want to play your games tonight?"

That's why the reindeer hated him, and they ran away to flee.

Rudolph the bloody nosed reindeer:

His reindeer massacre went down in history.

Snowman by Scott Deegan

I watched him with that snowman all winter long, ever since she left him. I tried several times to break the ice sort of speak, but he was pretty closed off. She really did a number on him. But the whole snowman thing was just weird, he spent so much time making sure it was perfect. I had to say it was a beautiful sculpture too, the man's an artist. That was winter, this is spring and he's still trying to save the damned thing.

I think it has to do with the blond hair sticking out of the head.

Tokyo Eve by Gábor Eichammer

Todd had a phobia of Christmas. As a boy, he sat in the lap of a man who smelled of alcohol and had evil eyes. His beard pulsed as he asked: Are you a naughty boy?

Todd cried. He became a lawyer and moved to Japan, where chimes played instead of bells and no red man descended from chimneys. Snow fell in Tokyo on the 25th. Todd came upon a fried chicken restaurant. A bearded southern colonel stood in front of it. It beckoned Todd closer, a familiar glint in its plastic eyes. It asked: Are you still naughty, Todd?

A Festive Bite by Gabor

Jiminy worked hard. He loved making wooden toys, and Santa was a good boss. Jiminy's only vice was smoking. One night, stepping out to light a cigarette, he heard something from the bushes. A wolf growled and leapt - yellow eyes and sharp fangs.

Jiminy woke up in a pool of blood, with a foul wound. Hiding his pain, Jiminy returned to his shift, then retired to sleep in his bunk. When Jiminy woke up, his bunkmates lay dead around him, their throats ripped open. Yawning, he went back to the workshop, the taste of blood still fresh in his mouth.

Seasonal Colours by Stuart Conover

Twas the night before Christmas when it happened.

Green and red were the color of the season. But this year there was no snow on the ground.

Instead, it was littered with the bloodied bodies of soldiers in uniform. A Red Army had invaded from the North.

Sneaking in they had no care who was naughty or nice. No one was left stirring, not even a mouse.

Deep in his bunker the President knew there was no recourse. Saying a prayer, he pushed the button. Within seconds the nukes flew.

It was going to be a white Christmas after all.

Necrosis Nick by Aaron Bader

The last N.O.R.A.D agent was hauled up and over the edge of the cliff with help from the team, finishing the arduous ice climb in just under two hours.

"No time to take a break everyone," the captain announced. "The crash site should be over that ridge. Let's go".

The fiery carnage of the wreck came into view.

"No sign of him sir, were goin-".

A trail of desiccated reindeer body parts lead into a cave.

"What the?" whispered the captain.

Weapons drawn, the team followed inside immediately immersed by darkness, and the haunting sound of gnawing.

Yule Match by David Simms

Our first Christmas together, yet I'm huddled solo on the couch, lips snuggling three fingers of Glenlivet as the flames begin to bicker. My other hand twirls the phone of my fiancé, his texts lighting the shadows of the den. My words, as smoldering as his had been, invited her for Christmas, now matched his howls of excuses. Their embrace ignites as quickly as their surprise had been, as did my smile.

The chimney breathed its relief, my agony exhaled, my eyes focused on the fresh kindling that soon curled together in ash.

I tossed their farewell to the yule.

Bloody Good Snowstorm by R.E. Sargent

I love a good snowstorm. The hill above our neighborhood is a great place to take the toboggans and inner-tubes. The excitement of racing down the hill at lightning speeds is a thrill unlike any other. Sometimes, after the snow has partially melted and refreezes during the harsh winter night, I take my sled down the slope.

Last winter, we buried little Jimmy's legs under the snow and jumped our toys over him as we reached the bottom of the slope.

No one blamed me for the accident; they never knew I sharpened the runners of my sled on purpose.

Tattletale on a Shelf by Shawn Klimek

"Scout," said the elf, stating his occupation.

"Let the record show the witness made "air quotes"," instructed the judge.

"Basically, I spied from a shelf, reporting naughty children to Santa. That was before I knew the perv actually prefers them!" he fumed.

"Objection! Conjecture!"

"Sustained."

"Without offering conclusions," coached the prosecutor, "please tell the court what you saw that night."

The witness pointed across the courtroom. "That pervert kissing a non-consenting minor in her sleep!"

"Objection!"

"How do you know what you witnessed wasn't the child's father giving her a good night kiss?"

The elf seethed. "It was my house!"

Yuletide Reunion by N.M. Brown

My ten-year-old son Charlie talked about a surprise guest for the entire week of Christmas. I ashamedly passed it off as an imaginary friend at first.

He never said his name; only to expect him for Christmas Eve dinner that night.

Despite the warning, I was still shocked to hear the doorbell ring. Charlie ran, squealing all the way to the door, and opened it.

Whoever was there stood just outside of my periphery as my son took his hand to lead him inside.

"Look!" He yelled. "It's Daddy!"

It indeed was his father; who'd died when he was four.

On the Wrong List by Benjamin Langley

Santa felt a prod as he emerged from the chimney, so he turned slowly.

"That's the last time I'm on the naughty list," Jimmy said, staring down the barrel of a shotgun.

"What do you want?" asked Santa.

"Let's start with candy and your word that I'll never be on the naughty list again."

Santa handed a few sweets to Jimmy who unwrapped one single-handed and crammed it into his mouth.

"You'll never be on the naughty list again," Santa said, smiling.

The elves always felt bad about lacing sweets with cyanide, but Santa insisted upon being

prepared for anything.

You Are On My Naughty List by Dawn DeBraal

Virginia waited for Santa Claus. She snuck downstairs in the middle of the night. She wrote him a letter weeks ago. Santa never answered. Virginia had a bone to pick with the jolly old elf. The reindeer landed on her roof. She stood before the fireplace as Santa came down the chimney, Virginia sat with her pistol in hand. Santa was pretty scared when he saw the gun in his face.

"Virginia, you are on my naughty list," Santa said sadly.

"It's ok, Santa. You are on my naughty list too." Said Virginia as she shot him in the head.

Angel Wings by M Ennenbach

The stone angel watches over her eternal resting place. A dusting of snow coats the acid rain pitted wings. The solemn face of benediction worn to a facsimile of loss. He sits in his car as the fat flakes fall against the windshield to drip down like tears. He imagines he can hear her over the heater. Her hands torn and bloodied, pounding the lid of the coffin. Her hoarse screams muffled by six feet of dirt and three inches of snow.

It has been two days since he interred her.

He smiles, his imagination plays.

"Merry Christmas my darling."

Milk and Cookies by Jay Bower

Santa demands milk and cookies, so children leave them out. One year, a child forgot to leave the offering and lost her head. Since that horrible night, newspapers and news stations send out alerts three weeks before Christmas: Make Sure To Leave Out The Milk And Cookies!

Parents assure their children are safe by guarding the milk and cookies until Santa leaves, protecting their children from a horrific end. He winks and nods and gobbles the treat, then up the chimney he goes, seeking the child who refuses to share.

Some nights the terrible screams are heard throughout the night.

Burnt Out by N.M. Brown

Our grandmother left us a string of Christmas lights nine years ago. Every year when we plug them in, each light shines radiant; eager to color the new tree.

Sometimes, a bulb burns out. Whenever this happens, a family member dies. First went Granny, then Pop-Pop; last year was the worst of all. We lost my younger sister; my best friend.

One year, I was determined to break the cycle. Relief washed over me the moment the lights reached the bottom of the trash bin. Everyone would be safe this year.

But I was wrong.

Instead, I lost them all.

Cat in the Tree by Scott Deegan

Joe looked up from his book and glanced at the tree. That cat was going destroy the ornaments by always climbing in the tree. He could see the tree shake from that goofy feline's play. Tammy would kill him if he let the cat break any more of her baubles. Why she spent so much on Christmas decorations was beyond him and how did it become his responsibility to make sure they survived Christmas.

"Tabby, get down from there." He said.

The tree shook violently and something shoot from it hitting the wall. Tabby's mangled body slid to the floor.

Revenge on Santa by DJ Elton

Christmas at Aunty Jo's. Billy and Jacinta, were restless, yearning to be elsewhere. Their aunt had set the scene well. Lots of alcohol. Every year, Uncle Perce was Santa, and the twins were his helpers.

'Watch me.' Billy said, wearing an elf hat, flashing a pair of handcuffs.

Uncle Perce was tipsy. His one last grope was Jacinta. As Santa touched her knee, Billy whipped out the handcuffs, snapping them shut before you could say 'HoHoHo.'

Jacinta taped Santa's mouth and eyes.

'No more Santa paws!'

They took the keys to his BMW and were off. Christmas was looking better.

Shiny Ornaments by Sea Caummisar

Shiny ornaments dangle from the green Christmas tree.
 Shiny ornaments make the Christmas tree so pretty.
 Shiny ornaments silver, gold, red and green.
 Shiny ornaments so fragile.
 Shiny ornaments made of thin glass.
 Shiny ornaments break so easily.
 Shiny ornaments crush so easily.
 Shiny ornaments I envision smashing in the faces of my family.
 Shiny pieces of shiny ornaments eating deep into their skin.
 Shiny pieces of shiny ornaments stuck in the faces of my family.
 Shiny blood on the shiny ornaments.
 Broken shiny ornaments dangle from the Christmas tree.
 Shiny blood dripping from the broken shiny ornaments.

The Giving Season (Part 4) by Stephen Cords

I gots no money so mommy told me to make her something for Christmas. That's cheating. Mommy bought all my paper and paints and glitter, so that's like giving her something she already has. I'm not a cheater, so I prayed for something to give mommy. God didn't answer that prayer, so I asked someone else.

He told me to draw a fancy star on the floor and he could help me get a present. I had to give him something, make a trade, but he said it was something I won't use anyway.

I hope mommy likes the bracelet.

The Goat of Christmas Past by Gábor Eichammer

There was a family, with crops, hens and a goat, which the daughter loved very much. The father loved his little girl, but one hard winter the crops failed, the hens froze, and when Christmas came there was nothing to eat. In desperation, father took the goat away and slit its throat, told his daughter the beast ran away. They all ate the stew, except the little girl. Later, in the candlelight, she wished for the goat to come back.

Father's stomach grumbled. Mother belched and fell. Intestines and flesh tore open. The goat came back.

A Christmas miracle indeed.

Dead Songs by David Simms

They arrived every Christmas Eve, songs resonating in my soul.

The children in discordant melodies, reminding me of sins past. Those seasons I took their wishes, their eyes full of hope and wonder, as they hid their deeds.

Yet I knew. The naughty list. They reminded me every December night, singing the carols they prayed would return their souls, and exchange mine in kind. Their words sharp as the knives I used, the choruses as tight as the garrotes I buried deep. they knew, always knew, that one Christmas the songs would draw me out, into their endless night.

Catching a Peep by Josh A. Murphy

Just after midnight. Officially Christmas morning.

She crept down the corridor, listening for any signs of him, growing more anxious with each step. Downstairs came sounds of movement.

Growing giddy with excitement, she tip-toned the staircase and peered through the living-room door.

Lights that coated the tree, like Luna Moths illuminated the room orange. A figure stood before the fireplace.

It was him; she was sure.

'Santa!'

The shape turned around.

Not Santa.

'You've been naughty,' it said.

She opened her mouth to scream but was silenced as a bag was thrown over her head and she was bundled inside.

The Ghost of Christmas Past by James Pyles

Bill sat at midnight in front of the Christmas tree; twinkling lights his only illumination. Six-year-old Emily died exactly one year ago. The coroner said it was an tragic, accidental death. His wife knew, but she couldn't prove it, so she left, taking everything.

"I'm sorry, Em. I know I did wrong, and I wish I could take it back, but…"

"Daddy."

"Emily?" Bill froze in horror at her specter.

"Be careful for what you wish on Christmas, murdering Daddy. I'm dead and I'm taking you with me."

The police discovered Bill bloodily impaled through his nethers by the tree.

Trimming the Fat by Dawn DeBraal

Bernie snuck around the tree just before midnight on Christmas Eve. He'd lost his job.

The factory shut down, and now he needed to "trim the fat." The pile of gifts going back to the store was growing. His wife, Edna, came in asking her husband what he was doing?

"I lost my job. We need to trim down Christmas."

Edna put up such a fuss.

Bernie looked at her flabby arms, and her loose jowls as she berated him for being a fool for losing his job.

Bernie put the presents back knowing now, where to trim the fat.

The Rubber Fish by Trisha McKee

Cindy leaned forward and wiggled her fingers over the wrapped presents. "You touch, you choose," their mother warned, her lips twisted in a smile. Cindy slowly unwrapped the package she chose. Smiling, she announced, "It's a doll."

Their mother nodded. "Exactly what you wanted."

Then Bobby's turn. He opened a package and burst into tears. Their mother clapped her hands. "You got the rubber fish!"

Still crying, Bobby made his way to the tub of water. He stepped in and immediately the fish started biting. As he screamed, Cindy ripped open the rest of the gifts, the danger now gone.

The Wild Hunt by Stuart Conover

Stories and myths are often based in truth.

This is something which Jacob knew all too well.

The idea of Santa is said to be hodgepodge of mythology.

Saint Nicholas is the most commonly one. Father Christmas, Sinterklaas, and Wodan were others.

It was this take on Odin that had Jacob curious. Or, that is, his relation to the Wild Hunt.

Years were spent finding where it occurred. Finally, he would stand witness to it.

However, he had been wrong. The Gods weren't hunting, they were being hunted.

Eternally.

After seeing the beast which stalked them... Jacob never spoke again.

A Not So White Christmas by Josh A. Murphy

White specks fell from the sky, covering the ground. His boots crunched as he walked, rounding the house with a bag draped over his shoulder. He paused to admire his handy-work. Another home ticked off his list.

With a content smile, he hoisted the bag, bettering his grip before moving on, aware of the need to hurry up. Behind him, the building continued to burn, golden embers rising into the cold nights sky before trickling back down to earth as charred white flakes.

The arsonist considered his stolen haul before picking another house to hit.

It never snowed in England.

A Parents Christmas Nightmare by Eleanor Merry

I bolt awake from an uneasy sleep covered in sweat. My heart is pounding in my chest and it takes me a moment to ground myself.

I'm in my bed. It's Christmas Eve.

I reach out beside me to see that Fraser is still snoring softly.

I breathe a sigh of relief and wait until my breathing slows before getting up to grab some water. I stumble into the living room and my eyes widen as they take in the wreckage strewn around the room.

The level of carnage and destruction is almost unimaginable and I gasp.

Fucking kids.

Springtime Surprise by RJ Roles

Kenny waited until nightfall to venture into the neighborhood. He hated Christmas. What's the big deal? Crappy music, cold, wet weather that made his nose snotty. No thanks.

Relieving his disdain of the holiday on all the festive decorations. He Smashed lights, kicked over nativity scenes. All while in sight of a lonesome snowman.

"What are you looking at?" Kenny asked the snowman, knocking off the carrot nose, and charcoal eyes. Kenny observed his path of destruction, when a coffin of snow engulfed him.

The next morning, a neighbor noticed the snowman across the street was now wearing clothes. "Hmm."

It Came Upon a Midnight Drear by Shawn Klimek

Through the shelter periscope, Sam confirmed that towering dust clouds of radioactive ash still rolled across the planet, coating everything gray. Nothing alive moved anymore. Only dead things. Reflecting on the date, his favorite Christmas carol to mind. Unfortunately, the brown-stained surgical mask he now wore had been acquired too late to save his vocal cords.

Even humming was impossible. To the unsteady rhythm of the zombie's stagger, he drummed on the glass and sang internally. With each beat, it's misshapen gray face came into sharper focus.

On the twelfth day since the apocalypse, my true love came to me…

The Peace Offering by Gabriella Balcom

"What's in there?" Kamina backed away from her ex and the gift he held out. "A snake?" He'd been downright vindictive after she'd ended their relationship, but she'd felt she *had* to because he'd abandoned white magic, delving instead into the blackest satanism.

Dalamar chuckled. "I brought you a peace offering since Christmas is almost here."

Kamina opened the present once he'd left. Discovering a box of five oversized, luscious chocolates, she ate one.

The others popped open while she slept. Two millipedes and three scorpions crawled out, all wearing Dalamar's face. Their eyes glowed red as they approached Kamina.

Why Santa Only Leaves Gifts for Children by N.M. Brown

My son Evan ran to the Walgreen's Santa; eyes sparkling and list in hand. He rattled off his list, hopped off his lap and grabbed a candy cane.

"And what would Mommy like for Christmas this year?" The man inquired.

Annoyed by the request; I answered.

"I wanna sleep in, not be asked countless questions, and be able to use the bathroom in peace. Can you do that for me Santa?"

Christmas morning, she awoke at noon… alone. All traces of Evan's existence disappeared.

Be careful what you wish for.

What's In The Box by Stuart Conover

Judy was always excited for Christmas.

The snow. The blinking lights. And, of course, the presents.

Even those not for her.

She knew all too well many weren't. Under the tree, the family's presents lay. Dwarfing them were those in ornate boxes. Presents her dad prepared all year long.

These were not to be touched.

"What's in the box?" she asked one Christmas Eve.

"The Abyss." He replied. "Nothing for good little girls. Not yet."

Later that night she peaked. Judy was never excited for Christmas again. Now all that mattered was preparing the boxes.

Filling them with The Abyss.

The Devils Fuge by David Simms

She locks the gaze just inches away, her face drifting to mine. A twinkle and a half-hearted grin seal the deal. I focus on them parting, more than the silvery eyes embracing me in her hunt.

It hung above us, the mistletoe sprinkled with the herb of her kind. She ached, it resonated in my chest, my heart pounding within her grasp. Lonely on the holy night, my lips betrayed my retreat. As hers opened mine, the needles within fed upon mine. By morning, I knew my love would dry in her arms.

With a smile crusted upon my face.

Just Say Thank You by Scott Deegan

"Really, Aunt Cassie? This isn't the one I wanted. This one is stupid." Elie threw the phone across the room where it smashed into the bar and fell in pieces to the floor.

"I paid $800 for that, I can't even return it now! What the fuck!" Cass looked at the fifteen year old and snapped.

The police arrived shortly after Eleanor's parents. It took them over two hours to remove all the Christmas lights wrapped around her. The star was embedded three inches into the girls head.

At her trial Aunt Cassie only sang 'Silent Night' over and over.

Hung By The Chimney by Scott Deegan

Four stockings hung above the fireplace, one for each family member. Starting with Daddy's they descended in size to the smallest, Jeffrey's.

That's how they were supposed to be the night Molly was home alone Jeffrey's stocking and Mommy's switched places. Perhaps it had happened earlier in the day and whoever hung them back up misplaced them. When she came from the kitchen however they returned to where they were originally.

She walk to the door and looked out the side window, no one. She turned to see the clawed hand pull back into the fireplace and up the chimney.

December 25, 1974 by Steven Bruce

Dear Diary,

Today I broke my one rule, no working on Christmas Day. One minute I'm in the park, the
   next, watching a family enjoy dinner. As I was leaving, I noticed the boy's lip-smacking. It triggered my misophonia, and I choked the little bastard with his mouthful of turkey. The living panicked and endeavored to resuscitate him. At his funeral, they'll say he's in a better place, but we know this is untrue. Tired now, will write more tomorrow.

Goodnight,
   Death

P.S. Please chew with dignity. Yes, you, reading this, thinking I'm a debt you can pay off
   later.

Christmas Dinner by David Bowmore

The family descend for Christmas Dinner. My brother, his partner and their two children.

Aunt Jules, Uncle James, their sulky daughter and her goth boyfriend. Mum and Dad.

My mother-in-law still thinks I'm no good, even though it was her son who had the affair.

My sister, Joan, and because her daughter, Evo, is also here, so is her ex-husband with his new wife. Not a good mix.

Evo thinks I'm 'Boring Auntie Sharon' but she should've seen me raving like a loon in '93.

No one considers the pressure I'm under.

I smile. Inside I scream.

This is hell.

I Just Want to Meet Santa by Wendy Cheairs

I just want to meet Santa

I wanted to see Santa, that was all. I tried staying awake, an amateur mistake when young. It never seemed to work, sleep always won. As I grew older, I would attempt to stay awake, waiting old, the mythic creature. I began to plan, no waiting to catch a glimpse. I retrieved items to collect my prize. Netting, locks, and bolts over the chimney trap on the rooftop for the reindeer to be stuck, even alarms with pressure trigger just waiting for a large man to come forth.

Now, I could catch my judge and jury of my life choices.

The Perfect Tree by Trisha McKee

Ryan followed his parents into the woods to find the perfect tree. As he walked, he thought back to the visit with the dollar store Santa. He thought of the words Santa had whispered to him, the orders he gave to him. As his parents shopped for discounted decorations, he was given explicit instructions.

It did not take long for them to find the fullest, greenest tree. As was tradition, his dad gave Ryan the ax to take the first swing. And he did take that first swing, right into his father's mid-section.

Because he really wanted that train set.

Wicked Choice by Belinda Brady

Ordering my beer, I ensure I'm loud enough to get his attention. He looks my way and strikes up conversation, like I knew he would. When I suggest heading to the alleyway for some fun, he jumps at the chance. Just like he does every year, with whomever he can get, his sweet wife unaware.

"I've been a bad boy," he whispers hungrily in the darkness and as my horns slide from my skull and claws sprout from my fingertips, I know my choice to pursue wicked adults instead of children this Christmas was going to be far more rewarding.

Christmas Feast by James Pyles

The elf Alabaster gathered all the children to the cemetery just after midnight when the Eve turned into true Christmas. Only these ten waifs still believed. The pale specter in green and red set them around Santa's gravestone. "St Nicholas, born 280 A.D. Died of Disbelief 2018."

"Please Santa, come back," sobbed six-year-old Latisha. Five-year-old Sammy wailed, "I love you."

A resonant voice rose from the grave. "Ho, ho. ho."

The Ancient Elf's hoary visage protruded above the Earth revealing hideous fangs. "Bring me my Christmas Feast!"

They ran, the echoes of their screams following them. So did Santa Claus.

Touching Decorations by Dawn DeBraal

Broomhilda was sad, now that Halloween had gone there would be no more eating little children stuffed with candy. She decided she needed to embrace other holidays. So Broomhilda went out into the woods and cut down a tree.

She put the Christmas tree up in her house. It looked bare, so she made her ornaments from leftovers and glitter. Broomhilda, clapped gleefully at the finished product. Her sister came into the hut.

"What is this?"

"A Christmas tree" cried the excited Broomhilda

"What are these?" her sister touched the delicate pointy ornaments covered in glitter.

"Lady Fingers!" Broomhilda replied.

Once Upon A Sleepless Night by Terry Miller

The Taylor's Christmas tree was always the prettiest on the block. Set up in front of the wide living room window for all passers-by to admire. It was quite the popular contest on Lynn Street.

Christmas Eve, little Brandy Taylor noticed something a bit peculiar about the bulbs. A strange glow within them slowly pulsed with dark shadows in the center, moving shadows.

It was 2 a.m., Brandy couldn't sleep. Sounds of chatter downstairs piqued her curiosity.

From atop the staircase, she peered into the living room where short troll-like creatures, hatched from broken bulbs, feasted upon her parents' bones.

Try Harder by Kris Kringle

Why do people lie?

It's not like I can't see what's going on.

They've even been told I'm watching them, but still every year's the same thing. I've been good all year bring me this, and parents encourage this charade. I mean I know it's hard to be good and really it's more of a percentage thing. If you're over fifty percent you're getting a gift.

This leaves me no choice but to let my brother know there are naughty children and unfortunately bad parents.

The kids will probably get a second chance, the parents are getting what they deserve.

Afterword

Thank you all for reading! If you enjoyed our little collection, please don't forget to leave a review!

Happy Holidays!

XX

Eleanor Merry

About the Author

To check out some of the authors other works, you can visit their Amazon pages below.

Eleanor Merry
Cassandra Angler
Alanna Robertson-Webb
Terry Mille
Chris Miller
Trisha McKee
Wendy Cheairs
RJ Roles
Stuart Conover
R.E. Sargent
Sea Caummisar
DJ Elton
Shawn M Klimek
Dawn DeBraal
Gabriella Balcom
Gábor Eichammer
P.J. Blakey-Novis
David Bowmore
N.M. Brown
David Simms

Printed in Poland
by Amazon Fulfillment
Poland Sp. z o.o., Wrocław

54914842R10082